BLACKTOP
TONI

BY LJ ALONGE

Grosset & Dunlap
An Imprint of Penguin Random House

To Freedom Fighters everywhere—LA

GROSSET & DUNLAP
Penguin Young Readers Group
An Imprint of Penguin Random House LLC

Text copyright © 2017 by Penguin Random House LLC. Cover illustration
copyright © 2017 by Raul Allen. All rights reserved. Published by
Grosset & Dunlap, an imprint of Penguin Random House LLC,
345 Hudson Street, New York, New York 10014. GROSSET & DUNLAP
is a trademark of Penguin Random House LLC. Printed in the USA.

Library of Congress Cataloging-in-Publication Data is available.

ISBN 9781101995686 (paperback)   10 9 8 7 6 5 4 3 2 1
ISBN 9780515158014 (library binding)   10 9 8 7 6 5 4 3 2 1

CHAPTER 1
SALTY COACH, SOUR PICKLES

No lie, Coach Wise even yells at me in my dreams. Which is not to say my dreams are edge-of-your-seat thrillers. I'm not one of those kids who spends all night riding on the backs of flying tarantulas. I never fall off seaside cliffs or wake up in a cold sweat, afraid of shadowy things lurking under my bed. I got enough problems as is; I don't have time to invent more for myself. Besides, you only find that kind of magical stuff in books with talking dogs or time-traveling closets. I don't even have a regular closet. Me and my older brother Roddy keep our clothes on a broken bookshelf left behind by the last person who lived in our apartment.

Anyway—I was telling you about my dreams. Mostly I just kind of walk around my neighborhood, living my life, eating fried pickles, until Coach Wise pops out from behind a Dumpster or bumps into me in a crowd and starts talking trash.

"This is what you dream about?" he shouted last night. I dropped a letter I was holding into a sewer. He has this voice, growling and deep, that makes me think of empty stomachs. "Running errands? Where's your generation's imagination?"

Every time I think about Coach Wise, I shudder. Not a practice goes by without him chasing me around the court, whistle propped threateningly in the corner of his mouth, ready to tear me to shreds. *Toni, go faster! Toni, you're killing us! Toni, why in God's name did you do that?* When things get really bad, he suggests cutting up my jersey, making scissors out of his fingers with childlike glee. I don't know why I make him so mad, but the one thing I do know is that you can't go through life letting people talk to you any kind of way. Doesn't matter who they are. Even Roddy has to ask nicely when it's my turn to do the dishes. Sometimes I forget or I just don't feel like it and I can sense him getting worked up, but if he says even a word, he knows I'll stick a foot so far up his angelic little— What I'm saying is that you get to a point when you got to stand up for yourself. You got to let people know you're not one to be played with. And Lord knows there's no reason to be scared of Coach Wise. His truck has not one, but two of those COEXIST bumper stickers. His forearm hair is thin and limp. When he thinks no one's looking, he rubs behind his ears and sniffs his fingers.

"Coach Wise," I tell him after practice today, "we gotta talk."

He squints unhappily in my direction. "Yes, Toni," he grumbles. It kills him to even say my name, I can tell. His arms are crossed security-guard style in front of him.

"I don't appreciate how you always yelling at me."

"Some people call that motivation, Toni. I'm a coach. I motivate." For some reason he opens an imaginary book, licks his finger, and pretends to flip a few pages. He points to his palm. "Coach. Definition: a person who helps others through sustained encouragement." He closes the book by slapping his palms.

Something strange and hot rises in my throat. Sometimes I have too many things to say and the words get so jammed before they get to my mouth that I end up sounding stupid. "So that means, like, what? So you think you're— So you gotta yell?"

A corner of his mouth twitches. He rolls his neck long and slowly rubs his temples. He says I make his brain hurt. He says he's never had a player so unwilling to follow directions. He asks if I think his instructions are just suggestions, open to any old interpretation. He wants to know why, for example, I get rebounds and dribble the ball up even though I know I'm supposed to pass outlets to Frank or Adrian.

"Yeah, well, I figured it'd just be better if I did it myself."

"But you always throw the ball out of bounds."

My face gets hot. I don't like to admit when I'm wrong, so I just stand there, silent and embarrassed.

"Toni, you're smart. Super smart. But you have a problem with authority. You think you know better than everybody."

"Says who?"

Coach Wise laughs. Did I remember the last game? When he asked me to pass the ball to Janae for the last shot? Do I remember what happened?

"You just stood there," he snorts before I can respond. Which is not *exactly* how it went down. What actually happened was that I got distracted by a fight on a far court. Two teams were pushing and shoving, and parents were coming down from the stands to break things up. An old lady got pushed to the ground and someone held up her wig on a stick triumphantly. JamLand is a facility with zero tolerance for fighting. You fight, you're out. By the time I'd turned my head around, the buzzer had sounded.

Of course he would bring that up. I can never win with Coach Wise. My eyes fill with water and start to sting. I open my mouth but nothing comes out.

"I want you to listen," he says, yawning. "I want you to trust your teammates."

He's so calm that I suddenly want to piss him off. He needs to feel the helpless, shipwrecked anxiety that I'm feeling. I picture myself grabbing Coach Wise by the ankles and holding him upside down, cartoon bully–style. I imagine secretly shaking a soda and watching him open it.

Instead, I just stare at him really hard. "You'll be sorry if I quit," I say. But I'm not even sure that's true. An embarrassed breath catches in my throat. I start to jog away before I can hear his answer.

In a cramped booth at Nation's, I trust my teammates to be as fed up with Coach Wise as I am. Justin and Janae sit across from me and make walrus faces with straws.

Frank asks Adrian to poke an almost-crusted scab as he winces and proclaims his imperviousness to pain. My battles with Coach Wise are nothing new to them, old stories with the same beginning and end, the same hero and villain. I decide to amp things up a little. I tell them that Coach Wise said he didn't want me on the team (maybe he didn't say that exactly, but he didn't *not* say it, either). I make his voice sound mean, snorting, Darth Vader–like. I use the salt and pepper shakers to show a few plays I've learned from TV, hoping someone will suggest that Coach Wise's plays are silly and outdated. I get myself so worked up, Frank stops slapping his scab to put a hand on my shoulder.

"It's okay, guys," I tell them, nodding

reassuringly. I look down at the menu and spot the fried pickles. There isn't a better fried pickle in the world, if you ask me. When I die, I hope they put pickles over my eyes and bury me in a pickle field. No—I hope they pickle me. I'll have to remember to tell Roddy that tonight: If I die, I want to be pickled. I'm a regular, so the waitress has already scribbled down my order by the time she comes over.

"And the rest of y'all?" she asks.

Frank doesn't want anything, and neither do Justin and Janae. Adrian and White Mike wave their hands.

"You guys don't want anything?" I ask.

"Not really," Janae says.

"Get them some pickles, too. You guys'll *love* the pickles. You'll be hungry by the time they come out."

I force a laugh, but everyone looks into their glasses.

"Anyway," I say. "I mean, do we even really need a coach? I mean, I just think we're smart enough to do stuff on our own."

Janae looks up and tries to smile. "I don't know," she says. She's smiling so hard, it looks like it hurts. "We kind of like Coach Wise."

The pickles come out in a big pile, steaming and crispy and sour-smelling. But by the time I'm down to the last couple, I look around the table and realize I'm the only one who's touched them.

CHAPTER 2

MORE FRIENDS, MORE PROBLEMS

Frank didn't wave to me when I got on the bus. Frank always cups his hand and waves to me real slow, like I'm a doomed passenger on the deck of the *Titanic*. It's the dumbest thing I've ever seen, but it sends Frank into such crazy fits of laughter that I can't help laughing, too. For the twenty-minute ride home I secretly pretend I'm at a swanky party on a boat sailing toward an icy grave. That lady asleep in her Walgreens uniform, she's a flapper; that guy taking up three seats with his gym bag, he's a tuba player. You're going down with the boat, buddy! At my stop I jump to safety, from the last step on the bus to my life raft, er, the sidewalk. But today Frank just walked away with everybody else, no wave, no nothing.

That probably doesn't mean anything, right? It's probably nothing to read into, but all afternoon I've been lying in bed, counting the rotations of the ceiling fan, trying to figure out what happened. Thin bands of yellow light filter through the blinds, cutting my body into strips. It's so hot, little beads of water drip down the walls. Hot air stings my throat and I occasionally bend my knees so that I don't feel so buried alive. I ask myself over and over and over why Frank didn't wave. Hours pass; I watch the threads of light move off my body and onto the walls. I've got four ideas: (1) Frank hates and/or is embarrassed by me because of that Coach Wise rant and now the rest of the team hates me, too, or (2) everyone's mad at me for eating all of the fried pickles and now they all hate me, or (3) they hate me because I missed every shot at practice, or (4) they hate me for reasons I don't know and won't ever be able to figure out.

If I said this to Frank, he'd call me crazy. We love you, he'd say. No matter what. He'd remind me that everyone is grateful for my job as the team's enforcer. Any time someone gets in Justin's face or steps on Janae's ankle, I jump in to make things right. Even Coach Wise marvels at the way I lustily pinch or elbow or otherwise punish our opponents under the referees' noses. I always get away with it; no boy's going to complain to the ref that he got hurt by a girl. White Mike says I'm like a kind of South American ant known for throwing itself into the mouth of an anteater to protect the nest.

"One tough-ass chick," Janae once said. "We needed someone like you."

I've heard other teams call us spoiled and arrogant and mean, but they don't know us from the inside. My teammates sit around and admire my crappy sketches of snails and turtles, like I'm some kind of big-time artist. They listen—they *really* listen—when I go on and on about how hard it is to draw realistic hands, how hard it is to get the nails right. When my brother Roddy works late, Janae comes over to play video games so that I won't be alone. Never once has she said anything about the linoleum pulling up in the corners or the mildewy smell Roddy and I have been trying to scrub out since we moved in. Over in the closet are the new Nikes the team pitched in to get me after I kept slipping and falling in Roddy's old cross-trainers. With the team, I always forget that I've spent my whole life learning to trust no one except myself, that the cartoons I draw know more about me than most people. With the team, food tastes better and the sun shines brighter and sweat smells sweeter and stupid jokes sound funnier and I feel about ten feet taller and nothing else matters, not the past or the future, only the just-tickled feeling I get when—

As usual, the more I think about how awesome Team Blacktop is, the more afraid it makes me. They're all so sweet and nice and good that I'm sure I stand out in some awful way, like a smudge on glass. Some nights I can't sleep because I'm sure that I've messed things up without even knowing it. Or I stay up wondering if the next morning is the one when they'll all wake up and realize that I'm not one of them, that I'm not the person they think I am. Maybe they'll finally see that my nose is too big or that my hair was dyed with the cheapo stuff they won't sell in a regular store.

Plus I've never been good at stuff like this—keeping friends and everything. Once I used a big plastic candy box as a snail farm. I called it Snail-o-Rama. I found snails right in the middle of the sidewalk and shuttled them to safety. Each one I named after a famous artist. I went out to the thicket behind our apartment and braved the thorns and spiders to get different kinds of grass and leaves, just to give the snails a little variety. That night I put the lid on tight. The next morning I popped the lid off and a smell like the worst kind of sewage hit me in the face. Rivera and Basquiat and Kahlo were all dead. I'd suffocated them.

I sit up, my arms and legs suddenly feeling tingly and restless. I open the window, and a blast of hot air rushes in.

Don't mess this up, Toni. Whatever you do, don't mess this up.

Frank forgot to bring his water to

practice today. I watch him suck his teeth as he digs into the corners of his backpack, pulling out his comic books, his sweatshirt, his mints. His lips look shriveled, like they've been left out in the sun too long. Poor Frank. I hustle over and toss him my bottle, hoping to make amends for whatever happened yesterday.

"Have some," I say.

He squints at the bottle, then shakes it. The water rattles weakly. There's a sip left, if that. The water creeps from one side of the bottle to the other. Slimy bubbles stick to its sides.

"Uhhh," he says. "I'm good."

"You're not thirsty?"

"That's all backwash, man."

I take the water bottle back and squeeze

it in both of my hands. "I wasn't trying to get you sick." The plastic crinkles obnoxiously, and I realize that I was yelling. "Sorry."

Frank stops looking through his bag and stands up. Even though he only comes up to my shoulder, I feel small under his gaze. A single bead of sweat drops down my forehead, over my nose, and into my mouth. I try to smile.

"You good?" he asks.

"Yeah," I say.

"You're acting funny."

"Funny how?"

He shrugs. "Just funny."

I look him up and down, trying to figure out what's changed. Hidden meanings sprout up all around us: the way he stands a little too far from me, the way he folds his arms over his chest. He glances at the ground, and I suddenly realize how giant my feet are, how clownish. Who would want to be friends with that?

After practice I get onto the bus slowly and head to my usual spot in the back. There's the lady in her uniform, talking on the phone about how they should have a separate bus for smelly kids. I stop myself from looking out the window, holding out until the last second, until the bus jolts into gear and pulls away. Frank's waving. His hand is cupped like a beauty queen's, as usual, but I don't feel better. Somehow he looks robotic, like he's doing it only because he feels sorry for me.

We've got an off day today, so I ask

Janae if she wants to get some ice cream. The sun is fat and yellow as it rolls up a cloudless sky, a glob of paint on a clean palette. At the Scoop-n-Serve there's a line of munchkins out the door and around the corner. Kids love the Scoop-n-Serve. In their commercials, a group of deranged toddlers plot world domination until they eat a spoonful of Pickled Cherry and settle for opening a couple of Scoop-n-Serve franchises.

I'm not exactly sure what I want from Janae, except that I want to be close to her, want her to like me. We get in line near a shady spot next to some Dumpsters. I watch her out of the corner of my eye, noting the way she bites her nails and walks on her toes, hoping that info will be useful sometime in the future. In front of us, two kids with no shirts argue about the correct way to fight off a bear.

"You run away," one kid says.

"Nah," the other kid says, "you're supposed to stand up to it and get big. Scares it off."

"Okay. You stand and I'll run."

Their bony shoulder blades flex as they slap at each other.

Janae practices her jumper in place. She catches an imaginary ball, sets her feet and rises, over and over.

"Jumper wasn't feeling good today," she says. "Felt a little flat."

"Oh," I say, shaking my head. "Weird."

What's nice about hanging out with Janae is that I never have to explain myself.

If I feel like being quiet, that's okay. And if I feel like talking, that's okay, too. We get each other. But now, as I watch her catching and shooting, I feel silly and invisible. I gelled my edges and talked basketball facts on the way here and she hasn't said a thing about either. She catches the ball, sets her feet, jumps, catches the ball, sets her feet, jumps, catches the ball—

"What are you doing?" she laughs.

"Huh?"

"You were copying my jumper."

My arms are straight up in the air, just like hers. I drop them down to my sides at warp speed. For the next few minutes we shuffle forward in silence.

Inside the Scoop-n-Serve, it's a madhouse. Chopped nuts and crumbled

Reese's Pieces litter the floor. A stream of vanilla ice cream flows like a waterfall out of one of the pumps. A sugar-crazed girl is standing on a table, shouting the Pledge of Allegiance.

"Nice and cool," Janae says. She does a fadeaway.

"Cookies and cream, right?" I ask. She'd brought it over on one of our video-game nights.

"Yup."

I grab two bowls and walk over to the pump. Nothing comes out of the spout. I pump and pump and all I get is hissing and sputtering and, finally, some liquidy cream. Now I'm panicking. I hit the strawberry lever, thinking maybe there's a kind of mix-up, *maybe* the cookies and cream is actually in the strawberry. But no—a thick stream of red ice cream comes pouring out. I whip around and there are the two shirtless kids who'd been in front of us. One of them has cookies and cream in his bowl, and now he's trying to ruin it with sprinkles.

"Wait," I tell him. "Is that cookies and cream?"

He holds a spoonful of sprinkles in the air. "Yeah."

"I need that."

He looks at his friend and back at me.

"Give that to me," I say.

The boys look at each other. The bones in the middle of their chests are almost hollow-looking. I look back at Janae, who's posting up a garbage can. Then I slam my fist into a tub of dried mangoes. The boys jump; their eyes are so big, you could trip and fall into them. A bowl of cookies and cream slides over to me.

"Thank you," I say. I head toward the register, but after a couple steps, I turn back. "Sometimes in life you don't get what you want." They nod their heads in sync. "Bears can run up to thirty miles an hour, so you've got no chance if you start running."

Outside, Janae and I sit under the shade of an oak tree across the street. Up above, a plane flies high and fast, making two perfectly straight white lines behind it.

"Good," she says.

"Good," I say. We scrape the bottoms of our bowls at the same time. We laugh. I lean back against the tree and savor the sticky sweetness of friendship.

Across the street, the two boys walk out of the Scoop-n-Serve, followed by two men with grizzled beards. They look down the street one way, and then down the other.

"We should go," I say.

"Don't you kind of want to just lie here and—"

"We should go right now!"

I grab her hand and we fast-walk through the park, leaving our bowls under the tree. I take big, awkward steps to keep pace with Janae's graceful stride. When we get a couple blocks away, we stop. I bend over to catch my breath, but Janae, who hasn't even broken a sweat, puts her hands on her hips and gives me a look that makes me feel about two inches tall.

"Not really a fan of littering," she says.

"Bad for the earth."

"Sorry," I say, surprised at how good I've become at apologizing. I can barely look her in the eye. "Really sorry about that."

This is what it's like to have friends? My whole life, I got along just fine without friends, and now look at me: literally stealing candy from babies. I'm not going to practice today. Frank calls and calls, but I don't pick up. It's time to get back to myself, to do what I do.

Drawing's the one thing that makes me feel like I know what I'm doing in the world. I sharpen enough pencils to create a little mound of shavings on my bed, then I pull out a sheet of binder paper. One day my art is going to be on the sides of buses.

On the sides of buildings, even. I'll be like Banksy, bounding across cities in the middle of the night, leaving rainbowed gifts while everyone sleeps. I draw what I like, whatever I can see from my window. With your basic Number 2 pencil, I can draw the delicate bags under a woman's eyes or the webbing of a duck's feet. I can draw the soft belly of a squirrel, the light reflecting off the surface of a puddle. Sometimes I spend hours just messing around in the margins, shading, tracing my fingertips, getting my thoughts straight. And the best part is that I get to be alone: no people to figure out or impress. It's just me and my thoughts, the way I like it.

There's nothing going on outside. From our place on the eighth floor, I can see the bay move in one long metallic sheet. A single pair of jeans blows stiffly on a clothesline across the way. I settle on a pigeon's nest in a storm drain a floor below. There's the usual twigs, but also a piece of a Nutter Butter wrapper, some Styrofoam, something that looks like a piece of a firecracker. It's like the pigeon's little pigeon brain can't tell the difference between what's good for it and what's not. Or maybe it doesn't know. Or maybe it doesn't care.

"Why build a house out of trash?" I ask the pigeon. It's one of those all-white kinds you sometimes see hanging out with the gray ones. It turns one glassy eye to me.

After two hours I've got no pigeon and no nest. Instead, I keep drawing a ball going into a hoop. On the street below,

I can hear someone dribbling a basketball, the pounding on the pavement like a drum. I look down the street and there's this girl, dribbling in a square from one corner of the intersection to the next. Suddenly I can hear Coach Wise's voice, telling her to get low, and I can hear Justin's and Janae's and Mike's, too. I crumple up the paper and throw it in the trash. I need to clear my head. I put on my shoes and head out to the Center to see my mentor, Ms. Cheng.

CHAPTER 3
WHEN YOUR HEROES CAN'T SAVE YOU

Roddy works at the Oakland Center for Happy Kidz. I guess I should say "worked"—today's their last day. According to a sign out front, the office will be turned into a Starbucks/hot yoga studio by next summer. By the time I get there, the party's over; the fruit platter is down to half a brown banana, and two kids with smears of chocolate all over their mouths are busy attacking balloons with plastic knives. Beads of sweat start to sprout on my lip; somebody's yanked the air conditioner out, leaving a jagged hole in the wall. A little stereo's playing Bob Marley when Roddy pulls out the plug. Suddenly it's just the kids screaming and somebody coughing miserably in a back room. Roddy throws the radio into a little cardboard box and slumps heavily into a chair.

"A Starbucks," he says, shaking his head.

If you've ever heard of the Center, congrats! It means you have a kid in your life with big-time family issues. Roddy's twenty years old, and we've been coming to the Center since I was in preschool. Back then we were bouncing from foster home to foster home, and the Center was nice because we got deloused, plus we got to see Ms. Cheng all the time. Ms. Cheng founded the place. Before the Center, I was a shy kid who chewed her hair and couldn't eat when other people were looking at her. But here is where I learned how to draw realistic-looking feet and learned who Basquiat was and learned that you should never, ever dye your hair with tomato juice.

As soon as Roddy graduated from high school, Ms. Cheng gave him a job as a counselor because Roddy's amazing at making people feel good. When we got sent to different homes a year ago—him to a place in the Flats, me to the Hills—he smiled like the world wasn't ending and reminded me that we Baldwins are like pigeons: We always find our way home. He's always had too much pride to cry in front of me, so he jumps up and pretends to clean. After he slides the fruit platter into the trash, he just kind of stands there looking at it.

A familiar yellow light glows from one of the offices at the end of the hallway. I find Ms. Cheng standing in the middle of her office. As usual, she's wearing a chunky necklace and bracelets and heels that make her look like she's about to tip over. But gone are her big glass desk, stuffed animals, and beanbag chairs she liked to call "safety bases." I've spent more hours here than I have anywhere else on earth, but it's all so weird and empty, I'm already having a hard time remembering what it used to look like.

"Sorry I'm late," I say, because I'm not good at this kind of thing, have never been good at this kind of thing.

"How was basketball?" she asks.

I can see Ms. Cheng isn't good at this

either—the good-bye thing—and that we're just going to play everything cool. She unplugs a lamp, and the room suddenly turns gloomy and gray. A jagged shadow creeps across her face. As I watch her carefully unscrew the lightbulb, I realize how stupid my friendship problems would sound to her right now. "Great!"

Ms. Cheng's one of the few people in the world I trust. Everything Ms. Cheng says, she means. She'll tell me that my hair color makes me look like a Disney character. She was the one who got me into drawing, who showed me the difference between sketching and doodling. She paid for four weeks of lessons with Frank's mom out of her own pocket so that I could learn how to use watercolors.

Now, she coughs into the crook of her arm. "Are you lying to me, Toni?"

"No, Ms. Cheng. I've got five new best friends."

"You're lying."

"I swear!" I cross myself. "Everything's great. Perfect."

I can see her trying to hold in a cough. Or maybe it's a laugh. Maybe she's laughing at the idea of me being on a team? All I can think about right now is if I'm Ms. Cheng's favorite. It's an annoying thought—I don't like to care what people think—but I can't help it. I want to be the one she thinks about when she walks out of here. But odds are I won't be. Everyone knows Roddy's her 250-pound angel. Before I know it, I'm angry.

"I'm gonna go now," I say.

Ms. Cheng takes an unsteady step toward me. "You sure? I could use some help with the rest of my stuff."

"Roddy's stronger, you should ask him."

I turn toward the door. If I look back now, the waterworks will start and I won't be able to shut them off. So I jog up the hallway, running almost, past Roddy, who's looking over at the empty Community Board, which used to have all of my old, awful acrylic paintings. Now it's just a strange constellation of colorful thumbtacks. In a flash I'm past that, past a stack of cardboard boxes, and I don't slow down as I slam the door open for the last time.

CHAPTER 4

LEAVE ME ALONE, OR ELSE

I'm fine. I'm absolutely fine and there's nothing wrong. And yet Roddy keeps asking what my problem is.

"Why do you keep asking me?" I say. I turn the TV up a little louder.

He tries to snatch the remote. "Because"—he gives up when I kick him in the ribs—"because you haven't said anything in, like, three days."

"So you're saying I talk too much?"

"That's not what I said. I said I've just been wondering what you're thinking, that's all."

His tone has a counselor quality to it, high and insincere. Even though he's got no job, he still gets up every morning, showers, and puts on khakis and a polo. He's set up our kitchen table to look like his desk at the Center. For days now, I've wanted to knock over his pencil tower and that pyramid made of Skittles. Now, Roddy sees me eyeing it and tries to nonchalantly block it from my view.

"I'm not one of your stupid troubled kids, Roddy." I get up and edge toward the dining table. Roddy flinches. One of the table's legs is shorter than the other and it wouldn't take much to make everything go crashing down. He turns up his mouth and takes a deep breath, and I feel sorry for him now—protecting a dumb table that he can't use for anything.

"You're sad," I tell him as I walk outside. "You're the saddest person I've ever met."

It's cool when I get outside. The sun's about to set, and everything's sad and blue. I should run back upstairs and get a sweater, but I'd feel stupid after just making a scene. I start walking to try to warm up, speed-walking through crosswalks, even when the orange hand tells me I shouldn't. I don't really know where I'm going. I could head up San Pablo, toward the park where I learned how to draw slides and oak trees, but I know I'll freeze after a few minutes. I pass a salon where ladies in curlers are watching ladies on TV, also in curlers, and their laughter trails behind me like smoke.

"I'm about to go get a burger with Ms. Cheng," Roddy says when I get back. "She said you better come. That's how she said it: 'Toni better come, too.'"

I kick off my shoes and yawn showily. "I'm tired," I say. "Long walk."

"You don't want to see her?"

"I'm just really tired."

When he leaves, I jump up to the window and watch him walk down the street. Heart racing, I calculate the amount of time it would take for me to put my shoes on and catch up to him. A bus obscures him at a stoplight; by the time it moves, Roddy's gone. After a minute I settle back onto the couch, flipping through the channels until I fall asleep.

I wake up when Roddy opens the door.

I don't know the time, but I know it's late; there's an infomercial on TV, some guy selling a set of knives that tell the time. I try to pretend I'm asleep, but Roddy plops down next to me. He smells like a strawberry milk shake.

"You up?" he asks.

"No," I say.

"Ms. Cheng was mad you didn't come."

"I'm not hard to find."

"You know that's not how she does. She doesn't force herself on anybody."

I sit up. "I'm up, okay? You happy? I'm up."

He tells me about what they talked about. He says she's moving to the desert to recharge and rediscover her inner voice. He says she found him a job at this new warehouse in Emeryville. Packing and shipping. Not glamorous, but it's something. He said she keeps running into kids from the Center on the bus or at the park, and sometimes they feel like they can't talk to her, which kills her. He takes a thick envelope out of his pocket and hands it to me. His eyebrows blast up his forehead.

"From her," he says.

I quickly shove it into my pocket. Twenty minutes later, as Roddy's falling asleep in front of the TV, I rush into my bedroom and throw the letter into a drawer. Then I lie down, heart thumping, and wait until I can't wait anymore. I turn the light on, open the drawer, and rip open the envelope. Small scraps of paper flutter into my lap. Some of them are so old, they're yellowing;

some of them have been smeared by water stains. I pick each one up. There's a drawing of a one-eyed dog, and a man-size lizard; a fist that breaks through the clouds to crush a house; an ocean wave that towers over an entire city; a spaceship that doubles as a flying squirrel; a snowman melting as it flies closer and closer to the sun.

Ms. Cheng always held on to these for safekeeping, figuring they'd be nice to look at someday, a way to appreciate how far I'd come. Now, as I unfold the papers and turn them around in my hands, I realize that I don't even remember when I drew most of them. They don't make me feel anything, not happiness or embarrassment or nostalgia. They're the map to a treasure that doesn't exist; I've got no use for them. I walk over to the window. The full moon looks like a peephole into another dimension. I toss all of them out and watch them flutter down like snowflakes. One of them catches a breeze and floats above the street, getting higher and higher on an invisible gust until it disappears over the building.

In the morning, I get up fast. I had a dream that I can't remember, but it made me change my mind. I want the drawings back now. I look out the window to see if they're still on the street, but it's too late. They've all been swept away.

CHAPTER 5

ONE STEP FORWARD, ONE HUNDRED STEPS BACK

Ms. Cheng says that art helps us get out the things we can't express—the "ineffable," she calls it—but for the last few days, all I've been able to do is sharpen pencils. Usually, I can look at a blank piece of paper and see whole worlds, things nobody else sees. In the past I have seen an angel fly into the flaming mouth of a dragon. I have seen a camel standing on the tip of a needle. But now? My mind's as blank as the piece of paper in front of me.

I haven't been to practice in two or

three days. This morning, I get a text from Janae.

> 9:38AM: U quit?
>> 11:50AM: Don't know yet.
>
> 11:50AM: What's up? Need u. Who's gonna make uniforms dope? :)

My fingers freeze over my phone. I'm scared to answer her. It's like there's this big canyon between me and her, and she's laid out this little creaking wooden bridge between us, and I have to walk over it. I want to. I grab a pencil and write cool, breezy responses that I hope she'll understand, something that tells her I need her without actually having to say that.

12:50PM: Feeling like crap.

Can't even draw a bird

12:52PM: Will see you in three

hours. Don't move

In exactly three hours, Janae is waiting for me in the lobby of my building. The sun shines big and orange behind her, like one of those medieval paintings of saints. I'm relieved when she doesn't try to hug me or put an arm around me.

"Come on," she says.

We start walking: a left, a right, then under an overpass, through a fence, and into a swampy auto-body yard. I step over pieces of half-sunken mufflers and severed car doors. We come out of the yard and into a narrow alleyway, where the sun can't get to; the sides of the buildings are cool under my fingertips. After a while I stop trying to keep track of all the lefts and rights, and I just follow. Janae doesn't look back, but I'm grateful to be following her, to have a big pair of muddy footsteps to walk in, to watch her ponytail swish hypnotically.

"Just a little farther," she says.

We walk behind a couple of boarded-up buildings: a meatpacking place, a butcher, a church. I realize now that we're in that old shipping yard near the freeway. We weave in between rusted train cars, all of them covered in two or three layers of graffiti, until I can see Justin and Mike and Adrian and Frank all standing in a circle. In front of them are big buckets of paint. Behind them is a train car without a line of graffiti on it.

I take a step back, my foot sucking up the mud, unsure of what I've walked into.

"Big-time artiste!" Frank shouts.

Janae says they carried all of the paint that they could from Home Depot. She says when I'm done with whatever I'm painting, people are going to see it in Idaho or Chicago or wherever these things go. "Go ahead," she says, "check out what we got." I crack open one can, a swirling liquid gold. Frank hands me a brush. I dip it into the paint and smear some against the side of the car. It drips down in long lines.

"All right," Janae says. "We know how you art types get down. Peace and quiet." She puts her arm around Justin. Everyone starts walking away.

"No," I say. "Stay. You should stay."

And so for the rest of the afternoon, paint flies. It dribbles down the sides of the car in silver and purple streams and gets smeared into strange peace symbols, alien lettering that we don't know what to make of. It ends up in our hair and on our faces, orange and green mixing on our foreheads and making a shining brown. Somebody shouts that we look like the kids in *Lord of the Flies* and that sets off a muddy, frantic chase over and through the train cars; we keep forgetting who's Jack and who's Ralph. All empty paint cans are kicked into oblivion. Before I know it, Janae's pulling me back to see what we've done. The sun sets behind a building, and suddenly we're in an orange, pulsing dusk. I look down at both of my arms, and they're covered in silver and red paint.

"What do you think, Toni?" Janae says. "You think the people in Idaho will love it?"

The truth is this is a train graveyard. The tracks have crumbled into little wooden pieces, the metal has been twisted and bent out of shape. These trains aren't going anywhere. But I look up at the train and realize that Idaho doesn't matter. We've done something I can't describe, a rainbow-colored mess that I couldn't have done on my own. It looks the way jazz sounds.

"Yeah," I say. "They'd better."

The next day I'm back with the team at JamLand. Streaks of gold and silver and purple run up and down my arms. I exchange secret glances with Janae and Frank, and each time we lock eyes, I get a little buzz, a little tingling I can feel on the back of my neck. I'm so excited, I'm skipping across the court as we get in line for warm-ups. Coach Wise watches me suspiciously. It's a couple minutes before our game starts, and I'm doing lay-up lines exactly the way I'm supposed to—catch the pass, take a couple dribbles, lay-up.

JamLand is basketball Disneyland. The lounge has three flat-screen TVs with cable and leather massage chairs you can use free of charge. There's a smoothie station and a shoe-cleaning station and an ankle-taping station. It makes the Center look like the inside of a cardboard box. The first time I came to a game, I took six Powerades, and Coach Wise had to sit me down and talk about professional etiquette. Today, I'm so determined to make the team look good, I only take two.

When the game starts, I sit on the bench next to Coach Wise. Frank brings the ball up the court.

Coach Wise stands up. "Run Elevators!"

I stand up, too. "Elevators, Frank!"

Coach Wise stops waving his arms to look at me.

I smile self-consciously. "Being a team player?"

Janae makes a three, and I clap hard. She gets a steal and a lay-up; I clap harder. Now Frank is dribbling the ball up court, waiting for her to get open off a double screen before throwing a bullet pass to her. The shot barely touches the net. Halfway through the quarter, we're up by a million. Coach Wise turns to me.

"Okay, Toni," he says. "You're in."

Out comes White Mike and in I go, to guard this scrawny kid who has to keep retying his shorts so that they won't slip down his waist. He looks so familiar, I can't stop looking at him, not even when we're on offense and Coach Wise is screaming at me to set a screen.

"You got a staring problem?" the kid asks.

That voice—I know that voice. "I know you from somewhere," I say.

"No, you don't."

I get the rebound and pass it up to Frank and I jog up the court with this kid, matching him stride for stride. His smell is familiar, too, something musky and mushroomy and sour, like old leather. "No, I know you."

I can hear Coach Wise shouting my name, but he sounds like he's underwater, a gurgling far away. I'm focused on the kid, on things that almost seem familiar: the mole on his shoulder, the way he walks on his toes. His name sits on the tip of my tongue, but I lose it every time he turns. He hits Janae on the elbow as she goes up for a shot, and the ref blows her whistle. Three shots.

"I didn't even do nothing!" he screams at the ref, and that's when I know. He's got a scraggly boy-beard now and his voice got a half-level deeper, but I know him.

I look at Coach Wise, who's giving me a thumbs-up from the sideline. I look at

Janae practicing her shooting form. I remind myself of JamLand's no-fighting policy. I focus on all the goodness I felt yesterday, how it felt to rub silver paint into Frank's hair. But my thoughts have turned soupy, and I can't seem to pick anything out from the muck. Something red and hard pulses behind my eyes. After my fist crashes into his jaw, it takes me a second to realize how much my hand hurts. I can feel it beating, can feel the blood rushing, can feel every nerve. I'm happy and dizzy as I watch him crawl away. It must be Coach Wise who grabs me from behind and whirls me out of the gym, muttering to himself that he can't believe it, he can't believe he just let that happen.

CHAPTER 6

WHY THE PAST CAN'T STAY PUT

I lived with that kid in a foster home last year. It was owned by a retired professor who lived on the top floor and only came down when a kid got sick or had a birthday. I remember pulling up to the place and swallowing my gum; it was an eight-bedroom castle in the Oakland Hills with a clear view of the lights in San Francisco.

Every morning you could go downstairs and eat cereal or fruit or toast. During the day you could sit at your bedroom window and smell drying wildflowers and eucalyptus.

Late at night you could hear families of deer wandering gingerly through the brush.

I hated it. For the first few months, I didn't take showers because I couldn't figure out how to turn on the hot water. The sheets on my bed were so cool and crisp—so much better than the itchy sheets I grew up on— that they'd keep me up at night. I missed Roddy, the way I could make the perfect pillow out of his chunky shoulders. And every time I walked past the fancy vases in the living room, I imagined accidentally shattering them into a million expensive pieces. And what if someone was watching me eat breakfast? And what if they tried to use that against me? I snuck dinner rolls from the table to eat at night in my room. The other kids were so nice—"Hi, Toni, how are you?"—that I didn't trust them. Most days I just stayed in my room.

I had started drawing again, little things like the leaves engraved in the staircase, the deer tracks near the garden. But after a while, the old pen I was using had run out. There was an art studio on the third floor that I found by following the smell of graphite. I walked by it every day for two months, my footsteps getting heavy every time I got close. A kind of force field that never let me just walk in through the door.

Then one day I saw one of the girls who lived down the hall with a set of sixty-four graphite pencils: seven kinds of blue, eight kinds of red, even a couple of those light browns you can't get in a regular pack. She was sitting on the patio, not even using them right—she'd mix red with gray, purple with green. I went over and asked where she got them from.

"The art room," she giggled.

"But *how* did you get them?"

She raised one eyebrow. "I walked into the art room. I picked up the pencils. Then I brought them out here."

Then she went back to drawing. She sat with one leg crossed under her. She had eyes like full moons and a mouth that always looked like it was about to detonate into a smile. I'd seen her before, laughing in one of the living rooms or making elaborate bacon sandwiches in the morning. She seemed free somehow, like she knew this place was hers, like she owned it. Right then I made up my mind to hate her.

"You wanna draw?" she asked.

"No," I said.

And that's how it went for a few weeks. I gave her the stink eye every time I saw her and she'd smile and wave back to me like an old friend. Instead of drawing, I took up working in the garden. I'd read *The Secret Garden* once and I'd always remembered the part where the guy breathes in fresh air for the first time and stands up out of his wheelchair.

First day I tried to tend the rows of corn and tomatoes. I spent about an hour brushing the dirt off everything. Then I unspooled a hose and dragged it across the yard and watered the corn. Five minutes later, my only pair of shoes were caked with mud. *The hell with this*, I thought. *Send me back to Danville, to the trailer home.* I'd kept my bag packed under the bed anyway. I kicked a tomato clear across the yard.

"That's not how you do it," a voice shouted from a bedroom window.

I looked up and there she was, the girl, her elbow propped up on a second-floor windowsill like a maiden in a fairy tale. I walked right underneath her. "So you're the queen of everybody around here?"

She clapped and her face got bright with surprise. "I look like a queen to you?"

I kid you not, her laugh bounced off the hills around us and came back scented with lavender. I got dizzy from it. Her name was Angelica. You know how it is with these things: It's always the ones you hate at first who end up becoming your best friend. She was two years older and had already been there a year. She had her own special couch in the library and the only room with a clear view of the Bay Bridge and a pet rabbit I fed deformed carrots to. She was addicted to laughing, would do anything for it. She had dimples like you wouldn't believe— these soft craters that I'd put my fingers in any time her face moved. Once, after the rain, I dragged her out to the garden and slathered mud on our feet.

"Oh *honey*," I drawled. At night, she'd been reading me Mark Twain stories. "Jerome is just going to *loooove* me after this pedicure."

"*Yes*, darling," she laughed back. "I doubt the menfolk will even be able to *recognize* us."

Memories are always a little brighter, a little sharper in the rearview. But if you asked me right now, I don't think I'd be able to tell you the names of the other kids who lived there. You could stand them right in front of me and I wouldn't be able to recognize most of them. Those were probably the best three months of my life, and even now I can only remember all the time we spent together in movie clips: girl meets girl; girl shows other girl how to plant tomato seeds deep so they stay rooted when it rains; girl lets other girl take Boardwalk every time they play Monopoly, hoping she'll like her more; girl starts biting nails like other girl and walking on toes like other girl without knowing she's doing it; girl grabs girl's sweaty hand and squeezes it when the coyotes howl in the night; girl doesn't know if other girl also feels electric shocks when they touch; girl cries secret, shameful tears every time other girl doesn't notice the cartoon vegetables she draws to impress her; girl gets better and better at swallowing her feelings, at keeping the bitter taste down and pretending everything's sweet.

She was a collector of things— butterflies, seeds, bees. When I told her about the Snail-o-Rama, she laughed and asked how I could forget to poke holes in it. One night we tried to catch bullfrogs in the tall grass behind the house. We split up, following two different frogs, but the moon was so bright, I could still see her dimples from across the field. The frog I was after sounded so close, I thought I was going to step on it.

"Toni!" she yelled. All the frogs went silent. "Come here!"

The moon had gone behind a wall of clouds. It was dark, and every time Angelica shouted to me, the breeze carried her voice one way and then another. Soon I was walking in circles, trying to find the moon, trying to find the path I'd been on. I sat down next to a giant root and took deep breaths to hold back my tears. I dug my fingers into the cool, wet dirt and listened for something. I tried to make out what the grasses were saying to the owls, what the frogs were saying to the crickets. It seemed, for a second, like the whole world was full of messages and none of them were for me.

Well, here came Angelica, zigzagging at full speed through the grass, beating her chest and yelling at the top of her lungs. When she got close, I stuck a leg out to trip her.

"Hey!" she said, rubbing her neck. She had mud all over her face, all over her mouth.

It was barely a kiss, a peck really, but I immediately felt bad. I thought I could feel her pull away. I groaned and dug my fingers back into the dirt.

"I got an idea," she said.

I don't know how she knew where the old man's whiskey was. We didn't do anything crazy, just a game of Monopoly and reading the old man's books in loud, English voices. We were sober enough to put the bottle back where we found it.

But in the morning, the old man brought all the kids together in the dining room. There was the bottle on the big mahogany table. He said he wasn't mad. He poured a little on the floor to show how not mad he was. He said he wasn't in the business of headhunting, but he would like someone to own up so that he could talk to him or her about responsibility. My head hurt like crazy, but I'd had a lot of practice over the years at keeping my face like a mask.

"Well," the old man sighed, "I guess I shall speak to each of you individually."

She was gone the next day. In her room was a kid who I'd seen slinking around the house and never talked to. Now he was smelling her sheets and rubbing his fingers over the windowsill to check for dust. I just stood in the doorway, trying to make him explode with my eyes.

"I didn't even do nothing!" he shouted at me that night.

After a few days I found out that not only had this kid told the old man about the whiskey, he'd said Angelica had taken the silverware and rare books. It was easy to go back to the group home after that— at least there was a chance of finding her. I trashed the art studio and got myself kicked out. They put me in a white van and dropped me off in a group home on Foothill and MacArthur, right at the bottom of the hill, where I could see the lights in the mansion go on every night.

That's how I found Roddy.

I try to convince myself that nothing happened. I punched a kid, yes, but they're not going to punish us for that. Coach Wise, I admit, seemed to disagree. He wanted to know if I was happy that I'd finally destroyed the team. He made me give him my jersey and swear to stay as far away from the team as possible. When I get home, Roddy is sitting on the couch, his knee bouncing up and down nervously. I almost never get to see Roddy now that he's started his new job. He leaves before it's light out and comes back long after the sun's set. When he gets home, he collapses onto the middle of the couch and falls asleep sitting up. Now, when he sees me, he jumps.

"All we do is pack," he says. "TVs, microwaves, PlayStations, laptops. You don't even get to talk to anybody."

Moments like these I'm reminded of the fact that me and Roddy were separated for a good five years and I'm still getting to know him. We live in a one-bedroom apartment no more than ten big steps from end to end, but I'm constantly surprised by the stuff I don't know about him. I don't know if he wants a hug or if he wants space, so I take two little steps toward him, my feet scratching against the carpet, and wait. "Okay."

"You don't even get a break. If you ask for a break, they remind you that the time you spent asking your manager for a break technically constitutes as a kind of break." Roddy looks down at his hands as if he's never seen them before. "I was in there today when I realized how stupid it was. Working there. Working, period. Look where it got me." He points to a blister on his hand.

I take another step closer to him. "That sounds horrible."

He smooths out the wrinkles on his shirt. Poor Roddy. Right now I'd be kicking something over, putting a fist through a wall, but Roddy's too kind for all that. His face is shiny and determined.

"I'll figure something out," he says. "I'll figure it out."

When I wake up, the house smells like Swishers instead of the usual gingerbread that Roddy likes. There are two guys sitting on the couch with their boots kicked up on the table. Roddy's sitting on the floor, a blunt in his hand. He coughs desperately after he takes a puff. Gone from the walls are the only baby pictures we have and Roddy's graduation picture. In their place are a couple magazine cutouts of women in their underwear, posing uncomfortably on cars and boats. I head over to the fridge for some ice.

"What I don't understand is," one of the guys says, "why they just don't make the whole bank out of the safe. Right? If you really want to keep the money safe, then you make the whole bank one big lockbox."

"Right, right," the other guy says.

Roddy nods but doesn't say anything.

The first guy turns around and looks at me. His eyes are big and red. He cracks his knuckles slowly. There's something wolflike about him, something hungry. "Oh okay, Rod. You didn't tell me you had a little sister. Now I see why! Looking that good. You gotta keep ones like that a secret."

"Ha-ha," the other guy says.

Roddy scratches his head. He starts to walk over to me and then stops so that he's standing between us. "These guys just came to hang out, um, we're just catching up and stuff. Ha-ha. We worked together at the warehouse and they hated it, too. You know. That's um, well, that's—"

"I'm Q and that's Booger. What's your name, li'l sis? Wait, wait, lemme guess. *Bonita*?"

"Your breath stinks," I say.

"*Spicy*," Q says.

I have to listen to them yap all day, even after I come out and tell them to be quiet. Q talks about his love for the great bank robbers, Pretty Boy Floyd and John Dillinger. He calls them *artistes*. He makes the sound of a tommy gun at the top of his lungs. Roddy says nothing, but I can picture him sitting there, nodding his head patiently like the good listener he is. Finally, they leave, and I can hear Roddy walking sleepily to my room.

As he's opening the door, I say, "The hell was that about?"

"Just some guys," he says. His toe grinds into the carpet.

Coach Wise doesn't want to hear it. Out of pity, Frank told me the team was meeting in Coach Wise's kitchen. I showed up unannounced and now there's a vein snaking across Coach Wise's forehead. It looks like it might explode if I move another inch. The team doesn't make a space for me to sit at the table, and I have to sit on the floor next to a large cactus. No one makes eye contact with me, not even Frank, who knows the whole story and already told me on the sly that he's forgiven me. He said I could tell the rest of the team and clear everything up in a second, but now, as I look at their scowling faces, I know

I can't do that. I'm afraid of what'll happen if I show them who I really am.

To no one's surprise, Coach Wise says we're suspended from the league. He runs through the options. He has already begged the JamLand CEO for forgiveness, to no avail. Zero tolerance is zero tolerance. Frank asks if we can't pay our way back in, maybe grease a couple wheels, but Coach Wise says what, we're the mafia now? We should go out and threaten people's grandmothers with wooden clubs? Besides, he put our uniforms on his credit card at 25 percent interest, so it's not like he's flush with cash.

White Mike suggests a petition. "What about the other teams in the league?" he asks. "Maybe they can vouch for us?"

Coach Wise shrugs, says why not, one

cannot be proud when one has hit rock bottom. He scrolls through his phone and eventually gives us each a list of numbers to call. I get on the phone with a Coach Heems.

"Hi, Coach Heems," I say, annoyed at the sugar in my voice. "This is Toni from Team Blacktop and—"

The line clicks. I look down at my phone and wave it up into the sky to make sure I still have reception. All afternoon we call: coaches, assistant coaches, other players. Everyone hangs up. Sometimes they laugh and remind us of how we've run up the score. We're getting what we deserve, they say. Boy, will the parents jump for joy at this news, they say. As the sun gets lower, we go from sitting straight-backed in our chairs to resting our heads on our arms.

Our voices get quieter, more pleading. No one wants us back in the league. We win too much, we're arrogant. One coach tells Janae he would sign the petition, but there's a girl on the team who abuses JamLand food and drink privileges. She glares at me, through me. How was I supposed to know they were watching so closely?

Coach Wise sits slumped in his chair like an old heavyweight fighter. He says we did good. He's going to order pizza as soon as he rests his eyes for a bit. Let him just rest his eyes. He puts his head down on the table. After an hour, Janae brings a blanket from the couch and covers his shoulders. We go from room to room hitting the lights, and then we walk out into the night, going our separate ways.

CHAPTER 9

BLOOD AND BOOGERS

Q and Booger bang on the door just as the birds start to sing. Roddy sleeps like the dead, so I let them bang and bang and bang, hoping they'll go away. But they keep at it. I put on the baggiest sweats I can find and open the door. Their eyes are bloodshot, and their faces are covered in scarves to protect from the early-morning cold. The summer's ending in two weeks, and you can feel the first bite of fall in the mornings.

"What's up, *Rob*?" Q says, fussing with Roddy's head.

Roddy wakes up groggily, using one eye to survey the situation. When he sees me, he shrugs shyly.

"Why are y'all even here?" I say. "Don't you work or something?"

"Easy li'l sis, easy."

"I'm not your li'l sis."

"My bad, li'l sis, that's my bad." Q winks. "I mean, Toni."

From under his jacket, he pulls out a grocery bag of hood ornaments. Mostly Mercedes and a couple silver ones I can't recognize. "Peep *this*."

There are maybe ten in there. He waits for me to say something, his eyes shining.

"You're dumb," I say.

He snatches the bag up and puts it back in his jacket.

"What you know? You ain't even that cute."

That's when Roddy perks up. "How come you're not at practice?"

I slap at Roddy, then head to my room for the rest of the morning. I can't draw anything good; my cats look like bears, my angels look like turkeys. So I just lie there. I don't think about anything. That's one of my tricks: To pass the time, you just close your eyes and picture yourself floating through space. Then you open your eyes, and three hours have magically passed. I learned that from Ms. Cheng. But at some point, Roddy shakes me awake.

"Hey," he whispers. "We're about to go out."

I grab him by the collar and pull his face

close. "What the hell are you doing, Roddy? What are you even doing?" He starts to shrug, but I stop him. "Don't shrug."

"No more hood ornaments," he says. "I'll redirect to something more wholesome. They're not bad guys."

"Roddy. Those are terrible guys."

"I think you might like them once you get to know them, Toni. I'm just trying to help them along, you know, be a kind of big brother."

Times like these make me so mad at Roddy. When he makes excuses for people who don't deserve them, when he convinces himself that he can save everybody.

Maybe we can get the Center back. Maybe if we get the Center back, everything goes back to normal: Roddy is in his right mind again, Ms. Cheng is back in her tacky skirts, I'm on Team Blacktop. I find something online that says you can get a construction project shut down if you find something illegal. When I get there, they've already put a chain-link fence up and ripped the sign down, leaving only the shadows of the Center's letters. Small piles of rubble line the front of the building. Guys in hard hats move in and out, and inside I can see a guy standing on a ladder, sparks falling all around him. I wave him over. He comes out to the fence, grizzled, his shirtsleeves pulled up to his elbows. He's got streaks of gray dust on his forearms.

"Do you even have permits for this?" I shout. "Where's your permit?"

"This for a school assignment?" the guy says. He flashes a big, friendly smile.

"Did they tell you there's a fault right under here? One earthquake and—" I make a kind of waving motion with my fingers.

He shakes his head. "What are you even talking about, kid?"

I stand there at the gate taking notes. A few hours in, I realize I don't even know what I'm looking for. The worst thing I've seen was a guy not put sanitizer on his hands after he left the porta potty. All the guys head home at dusk, looking dusty and beaten. One of them puts a hulking lock on the gate behind him.

I come back at night. It's all quiet except for a tarp crackling in the breeze. There are big yellow DO NOT ENTER signs posted every couple feet. I've got no plan; the best idea I've got is to take a bunch of pictures, send them to the news, and pray something happens. I wrap my hands around the chain-link fence, letting the cold seep into my fingers. Suddenly I'm climbing. My feet are a couple inches off the ground, and then a foot, and then two feet. I try to swing one leg over the top, but I can't. I'm too tired. On the way back down, I cut my hand on something sharp and now blood drips everywhere, all over the fence and the sign and the pile of rocks.

I need Band-Aids. There's a corner store a couple blocks down. When I get close, I see Roddy and his friends sitting on the curb outside. Roddy laughs when the others laugh, but it's not Roddy's laugh, there's nothing liquid or bright in it. It sounds more like someone's forcing him to laugh, like a laugh track. An old man gets out of his car and walks toward the store and all the boys jump up and block it. Q starts waving his arms wildly. The old guy looks back and forth between his car and the store. Finally he digs into his pocket and hands something to Q. Roddy slides aside and bows and opens the door for the guy.

I duck behind a telephone pole, run across the street, and head home. I run into the can lady a couple blocks from my house. Normally I'd avoid her, but I can see a ball of plastic bags in her cart.

"Miss," I say, "can I get one of those for my hand?"

"Sure, sweetie," she says. "That'll be three hundred dollars."

"Huh?"

She looks down at my hand. It's dripping pretty good, maybe a drop per second. "Three fifty."

"How can you charge three hundred and fifty dollars for a grocery bag?"

She opens her arms wide. "Look around you, baby! Prices going up up up all around! Three dollars for the bus and it don't even go nowhere! This is pie! Who are you to deny me my piece of the pie?!"

Just then a plastic bag blows by, and before I can take a step, she's reached out and stabbed it with a kind of wooden poker.

"Here's a fresh one. Three seventy-five."

I start walking again.

"Get your piece!" she shouts. "Get your piece!"

Coach Wise has good news and bad news; which do we want to hear first?

"Bad news," Janae says.

"I think I'll start with the good news." Coach Wise clears his throat. The good news is that he talked to some people, some very generous people, and we'll be allowed back into the league.

No one wants to ask the bad news, so we stay quiet.

"The bad news," Coach Wise says, "is that we won't be able to reenter the league as a team. They think it'd be best if we—they said it was the only way."

"We can't play together?" Justin asks.

"We break up the team, they'll let you back in." Coach Wise scratches the back of his neck. "The price of success, ha-ha. They want us to break up any criminal element by dispersing us, is their reasoning. Additionally, I'm permanently banished. They say I'm not responsible enough to control a team of youths. The technical term is called 'lack of institutional control.'"

Frank bends over like he's just been punched in the gut. "Nope," Frank says. "No way."

"But really the joke's on them, ha-ha." Coach Wise's lip trembles. "Because we are getting back together. But this is more of a probation-type of situation. You play on another team for a year, you get some of their discipline, and next summer we can get back together. So for the future of the team, we should do it. For me, you should do it. I don't want you to suffer just because of me." He pauses to look at me. "So you all go ahead. Coach Wise will be just fine."

As everyone leaves, I stay seated at Coach Wise's kitchen table.

"You want to know if you can come back next summer," he says.

I clasp my hands together. "I swear, Coach Wise, you don't understand, I—"

"Ask your teammates." He turns his back to me. "Ex-teammates."

My first practice with Dribster is in an

air-conditioned gym in Emeryville. It took two buses to get here, which, as far as these things go, is two buses too many. The coach shows up late. He has muttonchop sideburns and wears a turtleneck even though it's a hundred degrees out. He gazes into an iPad as he talks about "disrupting" the game and "maxing our on-court efficiencies." The other kids nod as if they know what he's talking about. I nod, too. I try to think about next summer, about running around with Blacktop jerseys again.

We wear electronic trackers during practice to see how much we're running. During practice breaks, we drink coconut water to make rehydration "more productive." I have to rub my finger on my throat to keep it down. I spend most of practice trying desperately to swallow my screaming.

"What the hell's he talking about?" I ask one of the kids at the back of a lay-up line. But he's got empty eyes: All he does is nod and stare like this guy's some kind of god.

"We're happy to have you," the coach says at the end of practice. "A lot of teams don't understand the power of technology, but with this team, we harness the power of technology for our advantage. I can assure you that no other team is playing basketball at the level we're playing it."

"Okay, right. But we didn't run any plays."

"No, no, no, you're thinking twentieth century. That's ancient, plays are ancient." Here he makes air quotes around "plays."

"We're not even thinking in terms of 'plays.' We're thinking beyond that. We're thinking cutting edge in terms of synergy."

He gives me a ride home in a car that drives itself. I grip the door handles the whole way and wait until he drives off before I exhale with relief.

The coach says we have to get to JamLand two hours early so that our bodies can adjust to the rhythms and energies in the building. He arrives just before the game and hands me a packet of grayish goop. I ask him what it is.

"It's to help get the synapses going early in the morning. It's a kind of oat-based energy supplement."

I pour a drop onto my tongue. "It's oatmeal."

"No, no, no. It's a proprietary-blended, nutrient-rich supplement. With oats."

We're playing Janae's team. She's warming up with them on the other side of the court. For a while she kind of holds the ball and looks around. Her uniform is too big and she keeps having to pull one of the straps back on her shoulder.

"Hey," I say.

"Hey," she says.

"How's it going?"

She bounces the ball once. I can tell that she's trying to decide how she wants to play it, if she wants to hate me for doing this to her or be friends because I'm all she's got right now. "It's weird."

"Same."

Both of us watch from the bench. The

kids on my team just kind of run around at ninety-degree angles until the shot clock runs all the way down, then someone desperately shoots a three. The coach slides over next to me and says this is what he calls "organized chaos." In my mind, it just looks like regular chaos. When Janae gets in, they play her in the post instead of around the three-point line where everyone knows she's comfortable. She gets bodied and elbowed down there and when they put me in, it's to keep her from getting rebounds she wasn't going to get anyway.

I kind of halfheartedly push Janae around and elbow her in the ribs. We jog up and down the court and neither of us get the ball because . . . boys. I don't care at all and I hope it shows. The game ends, we lose by thirty, and Janae and I didn't touch the ball in the last twenty minutes.

"Well," I say. "See ya."

But she doesn't say anything back. Coach comes jogging up to me as if we'd just won something.

"Look, Toni—for a girl, I have to say, excellent stuff, really quality."

"I sucked."

"Right, but, er, given your constraints? I thought it was a job well done."

I laugh. It's not like I've never heard something like this before. But I laugh and laugh and laugh, walking away, laughing until my lungs hurt, until I can't breathe, until there's water filling my eyes up to the brim and rolling down my cheeks and I can't tell what's going on, if I'm laughing or if I'm crying, as if right now I'd actually be able to tell the difference between the two.

In the following days, I see Frank, who's basically been made into a ball boy for his team. He pretends not to see me and I can't blame him. Adrian sits at the end of the bench by himself, drawing dragons engulfing me in flames on a whiteboard and then holding it up for me to see. White Mike's coach makes him wear lots of spandex and call out plays in his old TV character's voice, to the delight of the parents in the stands.

Roddy says Q and Booger are inviting us roller-skating and there is no saying no. On the way out, Q holds the door open for me with annoying chivalry. Roddy has a grill on his bottom teeth that he bought with the hood ornament money, but as we walk, he keeps taking it out to rub his gums.

The skate rink is nothing special: It's got that seventies wood grain and strobe lights that throw milky rainbows over everything. Marvin Gaye plays on a loop, and the whole place smells of stale popcorn.

A flashing sign says drinks are two for one tonight. In the corners between the strobe lights, couples make out in a ghostly dark. Now you see them, now you don't.

Usually, Roddy skates like an Olympian—figure eights and spins, the whole nine—but in front of Q and Booger, he plays the fool and goes slow, sometimes pretending to fall a little for laughs. His plan for changing the hearts of Q and Booger doesn't seem to be going well. I stumble and wobble over my skates, holding on to the sides of the walls. Who actually thinks this is fun?

There's another guy in front of me holding on to the wall, and I can't get around him. With one hand he holds on to the wall, and with another he holds a tray of drinks. His skates move under him in wobbling six-inch circles. Then he stops. He pulls out a notepad and scans the room.

"Excuse me," I say as I go around him.

"Sorry," he says.

"Coach Wise?"

His eyes get big. "Oh, hi, Toni. Hey there."

A table of middle-aged ladies with big hair scream lyrics to a Mariah Carey song only they can hear. He hands a drink to a lady who wants to know why the drinks are coming so slow, if they're flying to Jamaica for the rum or what. Coach Wise says he's sorry, he'll ensure that it doesn't happen again and he'll make the next round on him. She says damn right the next round is on him if he knows what's good for him. She tells him to bend down so she can rub his bald head. He bends down and she rubs his bald head. The whole table erupts.

Coach Wise chuckles. His name tag flashes in the lights—Abraham. "Very passionate customers here."

"Have you been coming to games?"

"Not allowed within a hundred feet of JamLand."

The strobe lights cast shadow after shadow on our faces. Coach Wise sighs. "You messed everything up, Toni. I'm going to tell you straight—you messed everything up. At least as a coach I could come in here every day with my head held high. I had something to look forward to when I got out of here. Now?" He drops his head, the bald spot reddish and raw.

I feel that like a punch in the gut. And

what can I say? "Sorry" doesn't do anything.

Instead, I help him pass out drinks. I refill the cups and take the empties back to the kitchen. I hustle like I've never hustled before. I grab his arm when he looks like he's about to fall. I man the register while he's repairing skates or mopping up puke or rocking the photo booth back and forth until it works again. Somehow him not yelling at me makes me feel weird. While he's stapling down some carpet, I tell him about a play I half-assed last game. I tell him about all the times I didn't fight over a screen on defense and forgot to defend the roller on a pick-and-roll.

I'm expecting something, his trademark vein, anything, but Coach Wise just asks if I can go to the kitchen and get more sodas before he gets in trouble.

"Trouble?" I say. "You're the coach. You don't get in trouble."

Coach Wise puts down his staple gun. "Can you stop calling me Coach? What, exactly, am I the coach of? Am I the Coach of Speedy Service? The Coach of Mixed Drinks? I am the Coach of Nothing, that's what I'm the coach of."

At the end of his shift, he sits down on a bench and unlaces his skates. The front and back of his shirt are dark with sweat. There's no one left but us and the boys. They walk out the front and I stay behind for a second. I ask Coach Wise if there's anything else I can do.

He says yes, I can not come back. He says I've already done more than enough.

On the walk home, I ask Roddy what all that was about, all the falling over like a clown.

"What are you even talking about?" he asks.

"You looked stupid."

Roddy fumbles with his keys as we get to our front door. When he finally finds the right one, he jams it into the lock. "You know what? Don't even talk to me about my friends. Like you got a million friends coming through." He sounds like Booger, like there's something in him ready to erupt, and for the first time I can remember, I'm scared of him. "You ruin everything. Stay out of my shit. I mean it. Tell me about friends when you actually find some."

CHAPTER 11
A MIDSUMMER NIGHT'S SCHEME

Today we're playing Justin's team. Before I can get away, Coach gives me a pat on the head and tells me to just try my best. Then he asks me to take a selfie with him. He says it's just something to show his friends on Inspiration Saturday. I wonder how people like this, who don't care about kids, get into coaching. They've got Justin playing point guard, which he never played for us. When he brings the ball up, he stops at half-court and holds the ball. He thinks for a long time about who he should pass to.

"Pass the ball!" someone yells at him.

"You can do it!" I yell at Justin. I get a look from everybody: Coach, my teammates, even Justin takes a backward glance at me. Old habits, I guess. But he looks somewhere past me, right through me. After the game, we're slapping hands in line and he skips over mine, like it's not even there.

"Come on, Justin," I say, but he doesn't look back.

I don't wait for the coach to give me a ride. I take the bus home and sit next to a guy who can't stop talking about how much he's going to eat for dinner. It's payday, he says. That means ham hocks and biscuits and mac and cheese and a turkey leg and a Diet Pepsi to ease everything on down.

When I get home, I fall asleep and that's what I dream of: enjoying plate after plate of food until I realize that there is no bottom, that the plates will keep on coming until I die. There are voices in the living room when I wake up.

"So what we do is," a voice says, and I can tell it's Q, "we just wait for him outside."

"Right, right," Booger says. "Wait like snakes."

"And then what?" Roddy says. I know my brother well enough to hear the fear in his voice.

"Grab him. Take him back in. Whatever. We'll figure that part out when we get there."

"But, but—" Roddy says. "How do we even know he has money?"

"Bruh. You didn't see all the coin from the skates? Plus all the money for the snacks and drinks? Weren't you watching nothing?"

They talk for a few more minutes, and then I hear the door slam shut. My mouth goes dry. I've got a million thoughts, but they're too slippery to hold on to. I feel like I'm floating, like I'm slowly being lifted out of my body and there's nothing I can do about it. What am I supposed to do? Roddy wouldn't listen to me even if I ran after him. Plus he's right: Everything I touch does turn to dust. Even when I'm trying to help people, I end up hurting them. Everyone I know hates me.

I look up at the ceiling, too paralyzed by dread to move. I try to count my breaths and fall asleep, hoping I'll be able to wake up and pretend this never happened. When I close my eyes, I see Roddy in the back of a cop car, both of his eyes swollen shut. I remember a conversation I had with Ms. Cheng. She told me she'd quit halfway through college and had been fired from her job as a chemistry teacher. She said every boyfriend she'd ever had had broken up with her. She said she started the Center because she wanted people to talk to, that's it. She would never say why she was telling me all this.

But suddenly I'm picking up the phone to call Janae. My face is hot, and I can feel my stomach get sweaty, and I'm full of that tingling relief you feel after you've had a close call. I'm pacing as I listen to the phone ring three times, four times, five times. No surprise that it goes straight to voice mail. I call Justin and Mike and Adrian—all voice mail. When I call Frank, it rings four times before he finally picks up.

"Hey," he says.

"I'm gonna need your help at the skate rink tonight. One a.m."

For a long time I can't hear anything, not even Frank's breathing. "What?"

The words are coming too fast. I have to force myself to slow down. "Coach Wise. Needs help. One a.m. Skate rink."

"Toni, stop playing on people's phones. You ain't gotta do all this to make people like you again."

For some reason I look at the phone. "What?"

There's another long silence. "If you want to hang out with us, just say that." The phone clicks.

I don't care. I'm a fighter, that much I know. Maybe not a very good one, maybe one that hurts more than she helps, but a fighter still. I'll go to the skate rink myself if I have to. I put on a hoodie and sneakers and wait for dark. For courage, I draw boxing gloves on my hands and a giant tiger on my forearm.

I show up to the skate rink around midnight. Coach Wise keeps wiping down clean tables and filling drinks for nobody in particular in order to avoid me. I fill myself up with ginger ale to keep the nerves down. Everywhere I look, the shadows and light are liquid, morphing into each other, making nothing look the way it really is.

At twelve thirty I wait outside under the skating rink's red flashing neon lights. The moon is full and high. It's the kind of bright dark that makes you see things, that makes you so afraid, little sounds turn into huge explosions. I scan the parking lot, looking for movement. A couple lamps throw down weak pools of mustard light. I see a shadow swiftly moving behind a car and hope it's Frank. It's just a cat. A couple comes outside, wobbling and holding hands and laughing as they climb into an old Lincoln right next to Coach Wise's truck. Once they leave, it's just me and Coach Wise's truck. I hear a loud thud around the corner, and my heart skips. I'm too scared to move, couldn't move if I wanted to. Finally Coach Wise comes outside. He looks surprised to see me, but then he turns around to lock the door.

"What are you doing, Toni?" he asks.

"You're about to open that door," a voice says in the darkness.

Three guys step into the blinking red light. They're wearing masks, but I can tell it's Roddy. He keeps trying to pull the bottom of his mask down, as if that's what'll stop me from recognizing him.

"Roddy," I say. "Roddy, I know it's you."

Roddy looks over to the other two guys, who are looking back at him. When we were kids, Roddy was terrified of this frog-shaped eraser I used to carry around behind my ear. It's the same look—kind of confused, kind of angry, but mostly sad.

"Who's Roddy?" Q says. "We don't

know a Roddy. Open the door right now, and everything will be all right."

"What are you doing, Roddy?" I ask.

Q turns to Roddy. "Roddy, I swear to God if you answer her—!"

"I don't know who Roddy is," Coach Wise says, "but either way, I can't let you in. I guess that's put us in a kind of pickle."

Q pulls out a wrench and takes a step toward us. It glints in the light like something fierce and ancient. Coach Wise and I back up until the metal door rattles against our backs.

Roddy takes his mask off. "Let's everybody just calm down."

Q stomps his foot. "Put your damn mask back on! There's cameras!"

Roddy puts his finger through the

mask's eye holes and shoves it into his pocket. I'm so proud of him, I could burst. But Q hits him across the back with the wrench, and Roddy drops to the ground, writhing and groaning, his arm contorted as he tries to reach the sore spot on his back.

"Open. The. Door."

Coach Wise puffs his chest out. I tell Coach Wise to just open the door, but he says, what, so we start unlocking doors any time someone asks us now? We start unlocking the doors to our homes and offices and hearts any time some bad man with a wrench demands it? He says no, he's taking a stand here. He's already had too much taken from him.

Of course right now is the time for Coach Wise to climb on his high horse.

Q shakes his head and pushes Coach Wise against the door. He swings the wrench behind him. I'm sure we're done for. I try to think of the few good moments I've had in life, pressing flowers with Angelica and unpacking boxes with Roddy and movie nights at the Center. Things were bad, but there were good moments. I'm lost in thought until I can hear something pounding across the blacktop. And then, faintly, I can hear Frank's crazy laugh.

"A wrench?" Frank says. He turns to Justin. "Dude brought a wrench to rob a place!"

I marvel at my buddies, at their untied shoes and baggy windbreakers and messy hair. Everybody's here. Justin and Janae and Frank and Mike and Adrian. They couldn't intimidate a sheep, but here they are, standing in a circle around Q, pretending like they're the baddest people in the world. I try to put a hand on Roddy's chest so that he stays down, but he sits up for a look.

We have Q and Booger circled. Booger says that if he's being honest, his mask is getting hot. He takes it off.

Q spins around to get a look at each of us. "It *would* take seven people to stop me," he says. He pushes past Frank. "Wasn't no money here, anyway."

Coach Wise stoops down next to me and Roddy. "You gonna be all right?"

Roddy turns to me and then back to Coach Wise. His lips are trembling, but his eyes look softer than they've looked in a while. There are tears rippling across his eyes. "Yo, are you gonna call the cops? Because look—I'm sorry. I can make it up however you want."

Coach Wise strokes his chin. "How tall are you?"

"I don't know. But I was always the one to string up Christmas lights at the Center."

Coach Wise extends a hand to help him up. "Good enough."

CHAPTER 12
FRESH START, PART II

Practice starts in five minutes. We're all sitting in a circle at half-court on this court spattered with seagull crap. The seagulls keep creeping back, and Frank gets up to chase them away for the millionth time. Justin says this is the court they started the summer on.

We had to spend an hour moving two Dumpsters off the court, rocking them back and forth, one inch at a time.

Roddy's sitting next to me. He didn't want to hear it when I told him this might be one of the hardest days he's had in a long time. Already I'm dreading the wind sprints and the dead legs and how much my lungs will burn and the fact that Frank will finish before me and rub it in my face and that there's no way I'll be able to wash out the metallic taste that creeps into my mouth when I get tired.

We're practicing even though we've got no games in sight. School starts in two weeks. Soon we'll be off to different schools and, if I know anything about life, it's that chances are good we won't see each other again. It's not really a tragedy—just another way life works. But you don't get used it. I've moved twelve times in my life—new friends, new houses, new schools—and it always hurts. There's always something ripped out of you.

It's getting dark early now. The sun sets behind a building, and suddenly we're in darkness. There are no lights on the court, and soon we can barely see the orange glow of the rim. There's a wind catching just the tops of the trees, a distant whooshing. Coach Wise asks us if we should call it quits.

"And go where?" Janae says.

For a while it's so quiet, I get spooked.

And then someone starts bouncing a ball, and without thinking, we start trying to play again, slowly, following the scraping of rubber and dirt and gravel, listening for our footsteps, just happy to be close to one another in the dark.

LJ Alonge has played pickup basketball in Oakland, Los Angeles, New York, Kenya, South Africa, and Australia. Basketball's always helped him learn about his community, settle conflicts, and make friends from all walks of life. He's never intimidated by the guy wearing a headband and arm sleeve; those guys usually aren't very good. As a kid, he dreamed of dunking from the free-throw line. Now, his favorite thing to do is make bank shots. Don't forget to call "bank!"